First series

Second series

Dark Man

The Dark Never Hides
by Peter Lancett
illustrated by Jan Pedroietta

Published by Ransom Publishing Ltd.
Radley House, 8 St. Cross Road, Winchester, Hampshire
SO23 9HX, UK
www.ransom.co.uk

ISBN 978 184167 419 3

First published in 2005
Reprinted 2007, 2009, 2011

Copyright © 2005 Ransom Publishing Ltd.

Dark Man

The Dark
Never Hides

by Peter Lancett

illustrated by Jan Pedroietta

Ransom

Chapter One:
Home of the Dark Man

It is day.

The Dark Man lies on a dirty floor.

Around him are bits of wood, all that is left of tables and chairs.

The house is a big ruin.

This is the Dark Man's home for now.

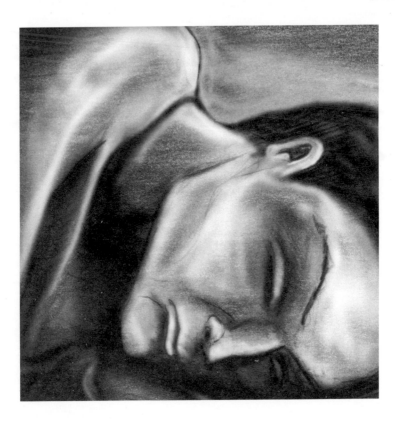

The Dark Man is sleeping.

Chapter Two:
A Time to Feel Safe

Daytime is when the Dark Man should feel safe.

At night, when it is dark, it is never safe.

Not in the places that the Dark Man
must visit.

Night is when the Old Man sends him.

Sends him to stop the evil work of the
Shadow Masters.

At night, the Shadow Masters are strong.

At night, the Shadow Masters can send demons who look like men.

Daytime is safe because the dark hides from the light.

Chapter Three:
The Dream

So now he dreams.

He dreams of times long ago.

In his dream he is a child and his mum and dad are there.

There is sun and trees and green grass.

Then the dark comes, very fast.

Mum and dad have gone.

There are demons hiding behind the trees.

Chapter Four:
The Dark Never Hides

The Dark Man wakes with a shout.

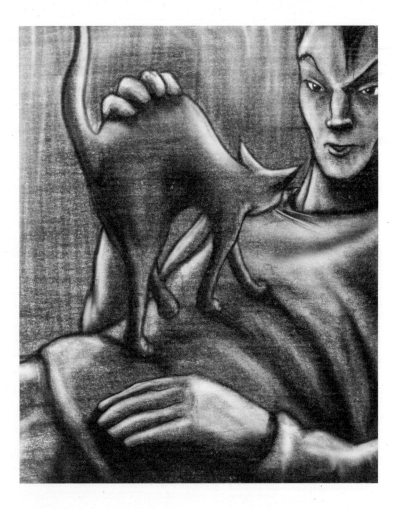

A cat has jumped on his chest.

He sits up.

It is still light.

Because of the dream, he knows he can never be safe.

The dark never hides.

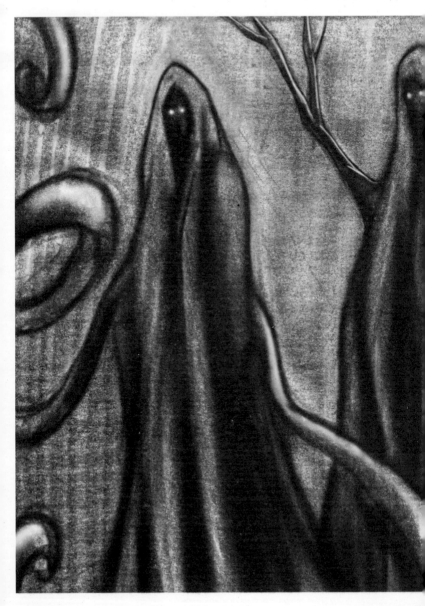

The author

photograph: Rachel Ottewill

Peter Lancett used to work in the movies. Then he worked in the city. Now he writes horror stories for a living. "It beats having a proper job," he says.